T·A·C·K Against Time

Created by MARVIN MILLER
Written by NANCY K. ROBINSON

illustrated by Alan Tiegreen

SCHOLASTIC BOOK SERVICES

To Becka and Katy, who wanted to help—
and did!
N.K.R.

ISBN 0-590-32406-3

11 10 9 8 7 6 5 4 3 2 1   4   3 4 5 6/8
Printed in the U.S.A.   11

CONTENTS

T*A*C*K is a secret network made up of four kids. We solve mysteries, everyday problems, and matters of life and death.

Here is what the letters stand for:

T* is my name, Toria Gardner.

My real name is Victoria, but please do not call me Vicky.

A* is for Abigail Pinkwater, my best friend.

Abby moved three hundred miles away to a town called Pleasantville, but we did not replace her when she left. No member of the T*A*C*K team can be replaced. She is now our Agent-on-Remote.

C* is for Chuck Finney, another trusted member of T*A*C*K.

K* is the code name for Will Roberts.

At first we called ourselves T*A*C*W, but it was quite difficult to pronounce. So we stole the "K" from Morse code (sounds like *dah dih dah*—long, short, long). In early telegraph language, "K" meant SWITCH TO SEND or GO AHEAD WITH YOUR MESSAGE.

Will Roberts's mind works like a switch. When everyone else has given up on a problem, Will's mind suddenly switches around, and he comes up with an answer no one else has thought of. He seems to be able to put things together.

Will and I grew up together. Even when we were babies, I recognized that Will's mind was special.

Here is my earliest memory of Will. We were sitting in high chairs once when we were babies. Will stuck the prongs of a fork onto a spoon.

"Foon!" he said. "Foon!"

The story goes that Mrs. Roberts then said,

"No, no, Willy. Spoon! *Sp* . . . *sp* . . ." She pronounced the sound carefully. She did not even notice that Will had combined the two.

"Foon," Will said, and he proved his point. Holding the "foon," he scooped up the mashed spinach on his little bear dish and threw it across the room.

But Will claims that his mind wouldn't switch around in the way it does without the rest of us giving him ideas. He says there's a certain magic in the T*A*C*K network.

We live in the quiet seacoast town of Sandy Harbor. Even in Sandy Harbor crime seems to be on the rise. We even had a case of sabotage this summer.

I do not keep this journal, however, to boast about the deeds and accomplishments of T*A*C*K. I keep it for practice. You see, I want to be a newspaper reporter when I grow up. I also want to own my own sailboat. I intend to travel around the world in it, covering big news stories.

I just hope it will be easier to be a grown-up reporter. Not only was I covering big news stories this year, I was right in the middle of them, as a member of the T*A*C*K team. It was quite hard to keep a clear head. We were saving lives, local businesses, and even children's birthday parties, but we were always racing against the clock!

This race against time started in May with our first town baseball game against our archrivals—the Monrose Monsters. I was right in the middle of that one. I play shortstop . . .

The Spy in the Locker Room

"Please stop tap-dancing out there, Rachel," Will's father called across the baseball field. "Right field is a very important position."

Rachel did one more little shuffle and a hop. Then she put her hands on her hips and whined, "Well, I think it's boring. Nobody ever hits the ball out here."

Mr. Roberts sighed. He is the coach of our new town baseball team. Next Saturday we play our first big game against our chief rivals—the Monrose Monsters. We have been practicing almost every day for the last month. Today Mr. Roberts has spent the whole time hitting balls to us to give us practice in the field.

On the next pitch, Mr. Roberts hit a fly ball right to Rachel. Rachel covered her head and ran away from it.

Mr. Roberts stepped away from the plate and looked over at Will.

Will has been sitting on the sidelines, reading a book about the history of baseball.

Will looked up from his book. "Is there something the matter, Dad?" he asked.

"Wouldn't you like to play right field?" Mr. Roberts asked him. "Just give it a try. Who knows? You might enjoy it."

Will shook his head. "I told you, Dad. I am very interested in baseball. But, you see, playing the game only confuses me. It is hard to see the true beauty of the sport when you are in the middle of it. To me, baseball is all strategy. It is all thinking."

Now, secretly I believe that Mr. Roberts only got the idea for a Sandy Harbor town baseball team because he has always wanted Will to play. Imagine his surprise and disappointment when Will announced at the beginning of the season that he did not want to play on the team, that he wanted to be bat boy.

"Bat boy?" Mr. Roberts was shocked.

But Mr. Roberts felt a lot better when his younger son—Will's little brother, Cyrus—turned out to be a good baseball player, even though he is small. Cyrus plays left field and is good at catching fly balls. He can't throw too far, but he is a fast runner. And when Cyrus comes up to bat, he always hits the ball.

"He has a good eye," Mr. Roberts says proudly. "And just look at that stance. Cyrus is going to be a slugger—a real slugger!"

THURSDAY, JUNE 4—

Two days until the big game! Our team is looking better and better.

I play shortstop, and Chuck, a trusted member of the T*A*C*K team, is an excellent first baseman.

Jill is a terrific catcher and a powerful hitter. A new kid named Colin plays center field. We all like him very much. He is quiet and steady—a good team player. Jerry plays second base. He's not bad, but he grumbles a lot because he wanted to be pitcher.

Everyone was surprised when Hugo Small was picked to be pitcher. He is not much of an athlete. He is short and a little chubby, but he has good aim. He always gets the ball right over the plate. My friend Emily plays third base. She is pretty good.

Rachel is our weak spot. Not only is she a terrible fielder, she is the worst hitter I have ever seen. She always closes her eyes before she swings. Naturally she always strikes out. But that's not the worst part. Half the time she stands at the plate and faces the wrong way. She faces the catcher instead of the pitcher. Then she says, "Oops," giggles, and turns around.

We have exactly nine players on the team, so no one is allowed to get sick. Will spends his time reading about baseball and putting linseed oil on our baseball bats. He takes his job as bat boy very seriously.

Mr. Roberts is not at practice today. He went to pick up our uniforms. His hardware store is paying for them.

Cyrus has been very fidgety all afternoon.

When he dropped his second fly ball in a row, I went out into left field to talk to him.

"Is there something the matter, Cyrus?" I asked him.

Cyrus shook his head, but his eyes kept darting around. He seemed very nervous.

Then he asked me if I had a comb. He said he needed to comb his hair.

"I never carry a comb, Cyrus," I said. "Please tell me what's bothering you."

Cyrus pulled me down and whispered, "Toria, is it true that scouts from the major leagues come around to watch kids play baseball? Do they hang around water fountains and make offers to kids when they see someone with a lot of talent? Someone who might become a big baseball star?"

I tried not to laugh. "Cyrus," I said, "This is small-town baseball. Who would send a scout to watch the Sandy Harbor Elves?"

Cyrus looked down at the ground. "I just wondered," he mumbled.

FRIDAY, JUNE 5, 6 P. M.—

Tonight we are having a pre-game strategy session in the girls' locker room next to our school gym. The whole team is here.

Mr. Roberts drew a big baseball diamond on

a blackboard attached to the wall of the locker room. He put x's around the field.

"First I would like to give you a few pointers about playing your positions . . ."

Just then our gym teacher, Miss Santiago, burst into the locker room. She will be the umpire at tomorrow's game.

"Harrison Parks, the editor of the *Sandy Harbor Herald,* is on the phone." She was very excited. "He wants to send a reporter and a photographer over tomorrow before the game to do a story on the Elves!"

Mr. Roberts seemed very pleased. He put his chalk down. "If you'll excuse me . . ."

"Dad." Will stood up. "Do you mind if I say a few words to the team while you're gone?"

"Words about what?" Mr. Roberts asked.

"The Care of the Baseball Bat," Will said.

Mr. Roberts shrugged. "Go right ahead," he said, and he and Miss Santiago left the room.

"First and most important," Will began, "never hit the ball with the label side of a bat. It may splinter the wood."

Will went on with the most boring lecture on the care of bats I have ever heard. As he talked, Will was moving around the room opening and closing lockers ". . . and it is important to weigh a bat every night. If a bat is left lying around, it may pick up as much as an ounce of dirt and moisture ..."

He stopped in front of the shower stall at the end of the room opposite the blackboard. Silently he slid his hand in, past the curtain, and turned the water on.

There was a terrible sound—halfway between a screech and a gurgle—and a tall, wet figure came stumbling out of the shower stall.

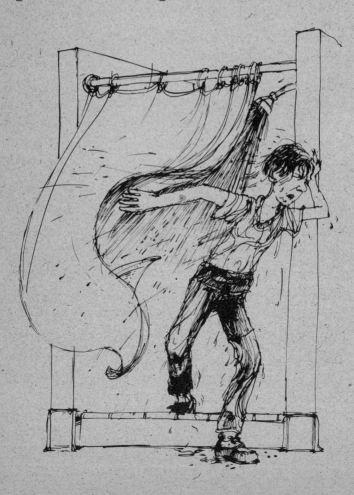

Will grabbed the figure by the arm.

"Let him go!" Cyrus screamed. "Don't treat him like that. It's the scout for the major leagues. He's going to make me very famous. He made me an offer yesterday at the water fountain!"

Cyrus suddenly clamped his hand over his mouth. "Oh, no," he whispered. "I wasn't supposed to say anything. It's supposed to be a secret."

"Cyrus," I said quietly. "That is not a scout for the major leagues. That happens to be the creepiest kid at Monrose. His name is Lester. Lester is a well-known sneak . . ."

Suddenly Lester wiggled his whole body just like a snake. Before we knew it, he had slipped out of Will's grasp and was running out the door of the locker room.

Chuck tried to catch him, but came back a minute later. "He disappeared!" Chuck was furious. "Lester was spying on us."

"Now, look," Will said. "The Monrose Monsters cheat. Cheating is their specialty. We should be used to their slimy tactics by now."

"We can't let them get away with this," I said. "Shouldn't we tell your father?"

"My father loves baseball," Will said sadly.

"To him, baseball will always be a clean, wholesome sport. I don't think we should ruin it for him."

THE DAY OF THE BIG GAME, SATURDAY, JUNE 6—

Everyone in Sandy Harbor has turned out to cheer us. My parents and my little sister, Holly, keep waving to me from the stands.

The reporter from the *Sandy Harbor Herald* asked us if we would meet him and the photographer in the locker room.

We had our pictures taken in our new white T-shirts with ELVES written across the front and in our new baseball caps with a little green elf over the sun visor. Then the reporter asked some questions about Hugo Small, our starting pitcher.

"He is not just our starting pitcher," Rachel informed him. "He is our finishing pitcher, too. We only have one."

"Oh." The reporter smiled. "And what is his pitching record?"

"He doesn't have a record yet," Emily said. "This is his first game, but we all love the way he pitches—slow and straight. It's easy to hit the ball. Besides, Hugo Small is very nice."

The reporter looked puzzled.

When we got back to the field we were just in time to see an enormous white limousine pull into the parking lot. It was a fancy car with silver chrome wings on the side. A chauffeur stepped out and opened the back door.

A very fat man in a purple satin outfit that said MONSTERS across the back stepped out of the car. He had wavy black hair and rolls of fat under his chin. He smoked a big cigar as he walked past our bench and looked us up and down.

"Who was that?" I asked Will.

"That's Dr. Rupert Underhand," Will said. "He owns the Dungeon Arcade—that big video parlor in Monrose. He is also the owner of the Monrose Monsters baseball team."

"The owner?" Chuck stared at Will. "Don't you mean the coach? The manager? The sponsor?"

"No," Will said. "Dr. Rupert Underhand calls himself the *owner* of the Monrose Monsters."

"That's ridiculous," I said. "You can't own a town baseball team. It's just a bunch of kids."

The Monrose Monsters arrived wearing real baseball uniforms—purple-and-white striped jerseys, and pants that reached below the knee. They even had inner and outer socks!

"They're going to win," Emily said. "Just look at those uniforms. They won't even have to cheat!"

Mr. Roberts met with the umpire, Miss Santiago, and with Dr. Underhand before the game to give them our batting order. When he came back to the bench, he said, "We're playing seven innings instead of nine, but other than that, the rules are exactly the same as in professional baseball."

The Monsters were up at bat first. Quite quickly they learned about Rachel's fielding ability. Every Monster started hitting the ball to her. In no time at all they had three runs!

There was a runner on first base when Red Jamieson, the meanest bully at Monrose, stepped up to bat. He hitched up his pants and swung his bat around in circles. He really looked tough. When the pitch came, he hit a fly ball to Rachel. The runner on first took off for second base.

I didn't want to turn around and watch Rachel run away from the ball again.

Suddenly I heard a thud. Our fans were cheering. Colin had caught the ball. He had run over from center field. He threw to Chuck on first base. Red was out and so was the runner on second. We had a double play.

"Two outs!" Miss Santiago called from behind the plate.

In no time at all we had three outs. And we were up at bat.

I was the first batter.

"Watch out," Will whispered to me, as he handed me my favorite bat. "Gretchen Messer is pitching."

Gretchen Messer happens to have a very scary face even when she's not glaring at you

from behind the pitcher's mound. I stood at the plate and watched her kick the dirt around the mound. Then she pulled her purple baseball cap over her eyes, glared at me some more, and blew a big pink bubble with her bubble gum. My knees began to shake.

Then Gretchen wound up and threw the ball—not overarm, but sidearm. The ball seemed to be coming right toward me, so I swung.

But just as I swung, the ball curved away from me and dropped down.

"St-r-r-ike one!" Miss Santiago yelled.

The next pitch was exactly the same . . .

By the end of the sixth inning, every one of the Sandy Harbor Elves had struck out twice. "That curve ball is impossible to hit," Mr. Roberts said.

Will's little brother Cyrus was the only one who did not strike out. For some reason he could hit that curve ball. But he always hit right to Red Jamieson on first base, so he was put out, too.

We worked hard when we were out in the field. Colin always played center field *and* right field. Rachel didn't seem to mind. The Monsters still had only three runs, but our fans were bored stiff. I saw Harrison Parks, the editor of the *Herald,* trying to keep his eyes open.

By the bottom of the seventh inning, the sky had clouded over. A few big raindrops began to fall. Our team was at bat—and it was our last chance.

I struck out right away, and Emily stepped up to the plate. Emily is a left-handed batter.

"If anyone can hit that ball," Will said to me, "Emily can. I read that it's easier to hit a ball like that if it curves toward you instead of away from you. You see, she's standing on the other side of the plate."

This time Emily *did* hit the ball. Red Jamieson fumbled it, and Emily was safe on first base. Our fans cheered.

It was Chuck's turn to bat, but he had to wait.

Dr. Underhand was on the pitcher's mound giving Gretchen "a little talk." He looked very angry. His face was dark purple just like his satin outfit, and his eyes were bulging out. Gretchen stared at the ground and sulked. For a few seconds I even felt a little sorry for Gretchen Messer.

Her first pitch to Chuck was an illegal pitch.

There was a big wad of pink bubble gum on the ball, but Gretchen told Miss Santiago that she didn't know how it got there.

"Last I looked it was in my mouth," she protested. "It must have dropped out by mistake." We all thought Gretchen would be thrown out of the game right then and there, but she only got a warning.

Chuck let the next pitch go by. *There was no curve on it at all.*

"Gretchen's shook up. She's lost her tricky curve," Will whispered. "Look at Dr. Underhand. He's booing his own pitcher!"

On the next pitch Chuck hit the ball right in the hole between the shortstop and third base. He got to first and Emily got to second.

It was raining harder when Jill came up to bat. Jill is our most powerful hitter. She hit a home run right over the right field fence! Chuck and Emily scored. The score was tied, 3–3.

Our fans went wild. I could see Harrison Parks jumping up and down on the bench.

Colin hit a hard line drive, which the third baseman missed, and got to third base.

"Toria," Will said, "they can't play baseball.

You couldn't tell before because Gretchen was so good."

By now it was pouring hard. Miss Santiago stopped the game just as Cyrus walked up to the plate.

"It's just a rain delay," she said to Mr. Roberts. "Take your team down to the girls' locker room and wait. This rain is supposed to clear up fast. We'll continue right where we left off."

The Monrose team was taken to the boys' locker room. As our fans were running for shelter, I saw a shadowy figure on the roof of the gym.

"It's Lester," Chuck said. "He's been sneaking around all day. Just ignore him."

In the girls' locker room, the Sandy Harbor Elves were in good spirits. "We're going to win," they were telling each other.

Chuck and I joined Will and his father, who were standing in front of the blackboard. They were the only ones who did not look happy.

They looked worried.

"What's wrong?" Chuck asked them. "We only have one out. We have a man on third. All we need is one more run to win this game."

"We're not going to get a run." Will pointed to the batting order posted on the blackboard.

"Cyrus might get a base hit, but he's not strong enough to hit Colin home. Then after Cyrus comes Hugo—and then Rachel."

I groaned. "I see what you mean. Hugo and Rachel can't hit anything. We'll have three outs and Colin will be stranded on third."

"Can't we change the batting order?" Chuck asked.

"Not in the middle of an inning," Mr. Roberts said. "It's against the rules. If the score is tied, we'll go into another inning, but we'll be in trouble. Everyone's tired and Monrose has their hitters at the top of the batting order."

"We've got to break the tie now," Will said. "And I think I know how to do it." Will picked up an eraser and carefully erased the board. "Dad," he said, "what about using the Suicide Squeeze Play? You give a signal, and as soon as Gretchen winds up for the pitch, Colin takes off for home plate. Cyrus hits that pitch—*no matter what.*"

Mr. Roberts nodded thoughtfully. "I see what you mean. Cyrus has a good eye, and if he *bunts* the ball just a few feet down the first base line . . ."

"Wow!" Chuck said. "The conditions will be perfect for a bunt—wet grass, muddy field. The ball will go dead! Before anyone can get to it, Colin will have scored a run!"

"But Cyrus will be put out," I said.

"It's a sacrifice play," Will explained. "It will only be the second out, and Colin will have scored the winning run. The game will be over."

Mr. Roberts was already clapping his hands and calling the team together. "Now, I want everyone to listen. Thanks to my son, Will, we are about to attempt one of the most interesting plays in baseball."

He drew a baseball diamond on the board. "Now," he began, "it's a lot easier if I diagram the play first. Then we will run through it. Colin—Cyrus—come up here."

We were all sitting on the floor in front of the blackboard when I got a tingly feeling in my hair. I was certain we were being watched.

I turned around and looked up. High on the wall above the shower is a slanting window, almost like a skylight. I knew at once why my hair was tingling. Lester's face appeared upside down in the window. A second later it disappeared.

I jumped to my feet. "Everybody stop!" I

yelled. "Lester's up there. He's on the roof. He's watching us through that window!"

Mr. Roberts looked up. "Don't be silly, Toria," he said. "There's no one up there."

Just then Miss Santiago called through the door, "The rain has stopped. In five minutes we will resume play."

Chuck stood up. "I'm going up there to check. This play has to be top secret."

"Hold it." Will stopped him. "It'll take too long to get across that roof. And it's dangerous."

"No one is leaving this room," Mr. Roberts said. "Besides, I'm sure you're imagining all this."

"Couldn't we climb up and put the shower curtain over that window?" Emily asked.

"Soap up the window," Hugo suggested.

"It's too high up," Will said. "It would take forever to find a ladder—especially a ladder that's tall enough. And we couldn't hold up a screen of any kind because of the angle and height of that window. Lester would still be able to see every place in this room."

"Three minutes to game time," Miss Santiago called through the door.

Rachel suddenly screamed. "I saw Lester's face. Just now! Oh, what a *horrible, horrible* face!"

"Now, now, Rachel . . ." Mr. Roberts said, but he looked less sure of himself.

"Wait a minute!" Will said. "If we can't get Lester away from that window, we can at least make sure he can't see through it. And I know how to do it. It will take less than a minute. Listen . . ."

We fixed Lester. Very shortly Lester couldn't see anything through that window. Try to guess what we did—before you turn the page . . .

The Spy in the Locker Room

Will's Solution:

Will turned on the hot water in the shower. In less than a minute, clouds of steam filled the room and fogged up the window. Lester couldn't see a thing. We ran through the Suicide Squeeze Play.

It was a success. Cyrus placed a perfect bunt a few feet inside the first base line. The Monsters were so surprised, Colin was home before Gretchen moved in to get the ball. Cyrus was put out, but the score was now 4–3 in favor of the Elves! The game was over!

Cyrus was a big hero. We all surrounded him and hugged him. At first he was very pleased. Then he suddenly said, "Hey, wait a minute. I got an out. Will that count against my batting average? Will it spoil my chances to make the big leagues?"

Will put his arm around Cyrus. "That is a good question," he said. "I am pretty sure that a sacrifice hit is not considered time at bat. Your batting average will not be affected. Come on, we'll go look it up in a book."

The Revenge of the Giant Worms

"You're not seeing that movie, Toria," my mother said. "And that's that."

The Revenge of the Giant Worms has finally come to the Sandy Harbor movie theater. It's supposed to be terrific. The ads on TV really make it look great. Will wants me to go with him on Saturday, even though he's already seen it three times.

"Oh, Mom," I said. "How can you do this to me? Every kid in my class has already seen it. I'm the only one who hasn't."

"The answer is no." My mother looked up from the book she was trying to read. "It will give you nightmares."

"Please let Toria go with me, Mrs. Gardner." Will was sitting in our den, trying to help me convince my mom. "You see, it's not just an ordinary horror movie. Deep down it's very philosophical. At the end you really feel sorry for these giant worms. They can't help it if they've been exposed to this radioactive rain and grow enormous and start to strangle towns and cities. And you ought to see the face of this giant worm right before he is finally killed. It is very moving."

My mother sniffed and turned the page of her book.

Will leaned forward in his chair. "It's a very serious movie. Don't you see, for centuries human beings have been unfair to worms. We trample them under our feet. We treat them like dirt. So you can't blame them for rising up against us when they get the chance."

My mother looked straight at Will. "Will Roberts," she said, "that is the most ridiculous thing I have ever heard." She burst out laughing.

Her book slid off her lap. "Treat them like dirt?" she gasped. "We treat worms like dirt?" She was laughing so hard she could hardly talk.

Will and I looked at each other.

"Can Toria go?" Will asked.

My mother nodded. Tears of laughter were streaming down her cheeks.

I waited for Will outside the theater. Kids were already lining up to get tickets. As I waited, I read the movie poster:

OUT OF THE DARKNESS OF THE SOIL THEY CAME, WRIGGLING AND SQUIRMING . . .

"Hi, Toria." I turned around. Will was standing behind me, wearing his best green-and-blue plaid shirt. Will has five shirts. They are all exactly the same plaid. You might say Will is a conservative dresser.

I grabbed Will's arm and pointed to the movie poster. "You didn't tell me that some of the worms in this movie were bloodsuckers."

"Well, bloodsuckers are worms, too," Will said. "There is no prejudice in this movie."

"Hi, Toria. Guess what I have in this box." Will's little brother, Cyrus, was standing behind Will. I was surprised he had been allowed to come.

"Mom and Dad let me come because I am doing a very important science project on

OUT of the DARKNESS of the SOIL THEY CAME WRIGGLING

worms," Cyrus told me. "Guess what's in this box."

I looked at the box Cyrus was carrying. It was just a shoebox with a rubber band around it.

"What a nice box," I said. I hate guessing. Guessing really bores me.

Just then I saw Chuck coming. He ran up to us. "Let's get in line," he said.

"How did you get your mom to let you see *Revenge*?" Will asked him.

Chuck looked down at the sidewalk. "Well, you see, she asked me what the movie was about and . . . well . . . I guess I told her it was a nature film."

"It *is* very educational," Will said.

Chuck looked up. "But I suspect the real reason she let me come is that she wants me to find out if she left her white scarf here last week. So I don't feel so bad."

We bought our tickets and went into the theater. Will and Cyrus went to find seats, and I went with Chuck to the Lost and Found counter.

"May I help you?" The woman behind the counter smiled sweetly at Chuck.

"Uh . . . my mother thinks she might have left her white scarf here last week when she came to see *At Long Last Forever*." Chuck was embarrassed.

"I wish I could help you," the woman said sadly, "but I'm afraid no scarves have turned up. Please be sure to let me know if your mother loses anything else."

Chuck promised he would, and we went to join Will and Cyrus in the theater.

Will was sitting on the aisle. Cyrus was next to him with his shoebox on his lap. I sat down next to Cyrus, and Chuck sat next to me. The theater was packed with kids.

"Toria," Cyrus whispered. "Are you ready to guess now?"

I sighed and looked at the box. "Let me think about it for a while, Cyrus. I always guess better when I have time to think."

The lights went out. Then loud, horrible, squishy sounds filled the dark theater. Titles flashed on the screen over pictures of bubbling earth. I shivered.

Will leaned over. "Now, Toria, pay close attention to this first part. It's very important if you want to understand the rest of the movie."

For the first fifteen minutes of the movie, scientists kept walking in and out of laboratories at some chemical plant. They looked at charts and satellite photos and said things like, "But if we keep releasing chemicals like that into the atmosphere, there's bound to be a reaction in nature." They used lots of big words.

"Hey, Will," Cyrus whispered. "When's the scary part going to start? When are the worms going to come?"

I was pretty bored, too. Then we saw a shot of a cozy little farmhouse. The beautiful lady lab technician from the chemical plant was sitting on a chair reading a book. Outside her window we could see rain falling. The rain had a greenish glow.

Then a shot of her garden in the rain, and loud, bubbling, squishing noises . . .

"Oh, boy," Cyrus said. He opened his shoebox and whispered into the box, "You're going to like this."

The beautiful lady went to the window. Suddenly she began to scream. The worms were on the rampage, wrapping themselves around trees. She escaped right before they strangled the whole farmhouse.

I peeked over at Will. He was peacefully watching the movie, but when I looked at Chuck, I was happy to see he was gripping the arms of his seat. His knuckles were white.

Soon the worms were taking over everything. There was even a river scene with a worm using a person for bait!

Then an enormous, whitish worm—the worm leader—slithered up a bridge in the harbor. People were waiting in cars to pay their tolls. Suddenly the whole bridge began to shake.

"Toria!" Chuck whispered. "You're screaming."

An Air Force plane flew over the bridge and machine-gunned the worm in two. Both parts of the worm grew rapidly. It was now two worms!

I hid my face in my arms and covered my ears to block out the terrible slithery noises on the sound track.

I peeked over at Cyrus. In the flickering light I could see his hand resting on the edge of the shoebox. Curled around his index finger was a worm.

I shrieked.

"What's the matter, Toria?" Chuck was alarmed. "Nothing's happening right now. The President is just having a top-level meeting to discuss the worm crisis."

I grabbed Chuck's arm and pointed. "Cyrus has a—a—a *worm*!"

"It's just my worm farm," Cyrus whispered.

"My science project. Sh-h-h, Toria. They're watching the movie."

I reached over and tapped Will hard on the shoulder.

"Will!" I said. "Cyrus brought worms to the movie."

"Yes, I know." Will never took his eyes from the screen.

Suddenly I felt something on my shoulder. It was the hand of a kid behind me. He was leaning over looking into Cyrus's shoebox.

"There are worms in there," he said.

"Get me out of here," a little girl yelled.

First it started as a whisper: "Worms in the theater. Worms in the theater."

Before we knew it, all along the rows kids were jumping up and down and looking under their seats for worms.

Cyrus looked around. Quietly, he put the lid back on his shoebox and put the rubber band around it.

"You've got to take that box out of here," I told Cyrus. "Right this minute."

"But I want to see the movie," Cyrus said. "I don't want to miss anything."

"I'll tell you what," Chuck said. "I'll take the box and put it right outside the theater."

"Someone will take them," Cyrus whimpered. "You can't leave them alone in some alley. I raised them myself."

"Look," I said. I stood up. "I'll take them to your house, Cyrus. They'll be safe there."

"You can't leave now, Toria," Will said. "You'll miss the end of the movie. Don't you want to know what happens?"

I sat down. I *did* want to know what was going to happen. Even though it was horrible, I simply *had* to see the end. I had to see those giant worms destroyed or I would never get to sleep tonight.

Just then a flashlight shined over our faces.

"What's going on around here?" The usher had a harsh, rasping voice.

All the kids were quiet. Meanwhile, on the screen the bloodsuckers were tunneling under the nation's capital, getting ready for a big attack.

As soon as the usher left, I heard a kid two rows in front of me say to somebody, "I think there's one just about to crawl up your ankle."

"Yikes!" screamed a girl way in the back. "There's one in my popcorn."

Will stood up. "I want to make an announcement," he said. "There are no loose worms in this theater. They are all in a box. And we are about to remove that box."

"No!" Cyrus said. "You're not going to get rid of my worms. You're not throwing them out of the theater. I won't let anything happen to Squiggles and Topsy and Screwball and Jack."

"Nice names," I whispered to Cyrus. I was trying to calm him down.

"Your worms will be perfectly safe. They will not go outside," Will told Cyrus. "I have it all figured out. They will be well taken care of and we can all watch the movie. I promise."

Cyrus handed Will the box. Will took the box up the aisle and out the door. He returned in a few seconds. Can you guess what Will did with that box?

The Revenge of the Giant Worms

Will's Solution:

Will took the box to the woman at the Lost and Found.

"I found this in the theater," he told her. "Someone must have lost it."

The woman was pleased to have the business. She put the box carefully on a shelf.

After the movie was over, Cyrus went alone to the Lost and Found.

"Did anyone find a shoebox with a red rubber band on it?" he asked politely.

The woman handed it to Cyrus.

"Here you are, dear," she said happily.

When we got outside, Cyrus sat on the curb and checked on his worm farm.

"They're all fine," he said. "And, you know, I'm glad they missed the end of the movie. They would have been very upset when they saw what happened to those worms. They might have gotten nightmares!"

Tick . . . Tock . . . T*A*C*K

"Whenever Abby comes, you and Abby go off together," my little sister Holly whined. "You don't pay any attention to me."

I was so excited that my best friend, Abigail Pinkwater, was coming for the weekend, I decided to start ignoring Holly immediately. I stared out the car window. We were waiting at the train station for Abby's train to arrive.

"Do try to include Holly," my mother said. "It won't hurt. And I have such a nice day planned. We'll pick up Will and take him with us to Stacey Cove. After we swim, we can walk up to Dragon's Mouth and pick some blueberries."

"Oh, Mom," I moaned. "Why do you always have to make so many plans? I won't get a single second to talk to Abby."

My mother was about to give me a lecture when, luckily, the gates went down. Abby's train was coming.

Sometimes it takes awhile for Abby and me to get used to each other. Abby seemed shy when she got into the car, but when we were waiting outside Will's house, I asked her how things were in Pleasantville.

"Not good," Abby said. "Not good at all. Wait till I tell you what this kid Kathy did to me behind my back . . . "

Right away I knew everything would be fine.

Will climbed into the backseat with us. He was wearing his hiking boots. He was very excited about going to Stacey Cove.

"Maybe we can watch the digging around Dragon's Mouth," he said. "Mr. Hawk, the director of the Sandy Harbor Historical Society, is working up there with a team from the university. They're looking for Indian relics."

I am quite interested in history, and I like Mr. Hawk very much, but I turned to Abby and said, "Well, why didn't you just tell her that right to her face. Sorry, Will, but this is important. We're talking about this girl Kathy."

It was a beautiful day at Stacey Cove. The beach wasn't very crowded. Abby and I sat on blankets and talked. Holly sat right between us and listened.

Mom and Will said they wanted to take a walk up to Dragon's Mouth Cave to see if they could watch Mr. Hawk digging for relics.

"Could Abby and I stay here?" I asked.

"Me, too," Holly begged.

"I guess so," my mother said. "But don't eat the picnic until we get back."

An hour went by.

"I think we could each have one sandwich," I told Abby and Holly. "She wouldn't want us to starve."

I was about to bite into a ham-and-cheese sandwich when I heard a rumble. I looked up. The sun was shining. There wasn't a cloud in the sky.

Then the sand beneath us seemed to tremble.

Abby was scared. "What was that?"

"I don't know," I said. "Sandy Harbor isn't exactly known for its earthquakes."

Other people on the beach had noticed it, too.

"Must be the blasting for the new highway," one man said.

"One of those supersonic jets," a woman suggested.

Abby, Holly, and I began to eat.

Fifteen minutes later I heard sirens. They were coming from the direction of Dragon's Mouth.

My hands and feet turned cold.

"Something's happened," I said. "Mom and Will are up there."

We put on our shoes quickly. Abby took Holly's hand. We took off down the beach dragging Holly, who was clutching her pail and shovel.

We followed the road that winds around Thief Hill. When we came to the ledge near Dragon's Mouth Cave, I saw the flashing light of a police car. It was blocking the road.

"Sergeant Small!" I yelled. I had recognized one of the policemen. I ran toward him.

He waved us back. "No one's allowed in this area," he called. "Get back."

I went up to him anyway. "It's me, Toria Gardner. My mom's up here." I was trying to keep my voice from shaking. "Please tell me what happened."

Sergeant Small blinked. "Oh, Toria, sorry I didn't recognize you. Your mom's all right. There's been a rock slide. She's up there with the rescue crews."

I looked across the ledge. I saw fire trucks and an ambulance waiting with a stretcher. Then I saw my mother standing with Chief Mulligan of the Sandy Harbor Fire Department.

"A big boulder fell in the rock slide. It's blocking the entrance to Dragon's Mouth Cave," Sergeant Small told us. "Mr. Hawk and three of his team from the university are trapped inside."

"Oh, no," I said. "Not Mr. Hawk!"

"He seems to be all right," Sergeant Small said. "But one of the students—a kid of nineteen—is in shock. Your mother is giving instructions to the people inside. She's telling them how to care for the boy. I didn't know your mother was an emergency medical technician," Sergeant Small said.

I nodded. My mother had taken a course this year. She used to be a nurse. She wanted to get up to date on the latest first-aid and medical-rescue techniques.

My head suddenly felt very light. I sat down on the side of the road and put my head in my arms. All I could think was, *Things like this don't happen in Sandy Harbor.*

I looked up. Holly was standing above me, patting me very gently on the head.

"Mommy's all right," she said. "You heard what he said. She's all right. She's just helping."

Then I heard Abby's voice. "What about Will Roberts? He was with Mrs. Gardner."

"Will was the one who called us," Sergeant Small said. "He ran down the road to the highway and used the telephone at the gas station. He went back to the beach to look for you."

Just then, I spotted Will coming up the road.

"I've been looking all over for you," he called to us. He sat down next to me.

Sergeant Small said, "Wait here. I'll go tell your mother you're all right."

"Wait a minute," I said. "What if there's another rock slide?"

"We've taken every precaution to protect the people on the site," Sergeant Small said.

"What about the kid who's in shock?" Abby asked. "Did he get hit by the boulder?"

"He's not injured," Sergeant Small said. "The shock comes from fright, but it's just as serious as any other kind of shock."

"Um . . . can you die of shock?" I asked.

Sergeant Small didn't say anything for a moment. I looked at Will. Will nodded.

"The most important thing right now is to keep him warm," Sergeant Small said. "Luckily, there's a small space all the way around the boulder. It's not big enough for a person to get through, but they managed to slip a blanket through the widest part."

Sergeant Small went to tell my mother we were all right. She looked around and waved to us. Then she turned back.

A mobile van from an all-news radio station

pulled up and parked outside the road block. A man with a press badge on his jacket got out and ran over to talk to Chief Mulligan and the other rescue workers. He spent a long time at the site.

When he came back, he said, "Is Will Roberts here?" He told Will he wanted to interview him.

He was very nice. He asked Will a few questions about the rock slide and the telephone call he had made from the gas station. Then he sat and talked to us. His name was Peter Barton.

"That boulder presents a tremendous problem," Peter said. "It's extremely heavy—too heavy for the people inside to push it out. They're having no luck trying to pry it loose, either. They've tried every kind of tool—you see those big jaws they're using right now?"

We nodded.

"Could they chip away a piece?" Will asked.

"They're trying to, but even if they had one of those big drills, it would just make holes in the rock. It would take a long time before a piece would break off. That rock is solid granite. And they're working against time."

Peter talked in a quiet voice. It was nice to know what was going on. Somehow it made the whole thing less scary. Holly took her pail and shovel to the edge of the road and began digging in the sand.

"Can't they move the boulder with a truck—a pickup truck or something?" I asked.

"They need a vehicle with more power," Peter told me. "The police have just put out a request on their radio for a wheel loader—one of those big tractors that road crews use. There's a road crew nearby and it's on the way here right now."

"Will they use the wheel loader to push the boulder into the cave?" Abby asked. "So the people can crawl out around it?"

"No," Peter said. "They are sure they could push it quite a long way into the cave, but the cave is pretty much like a tunnel. It doesn't get wider. The people would just be trapped farther back in the cave."

"So are they going to try to pull it out?" Will asked.

"Yes," Peter said. He stood up. "There's the wheel loader now."

The wheel loader did look like an enormous

tractor. We watched as it made several attempts to get a grip on the top of the boulder with the teeth of its scoop.

"If the teeth hold, the driver will back up the wheel loader and try to pull the boulder away from the entrance to the cave," Peter said.

Just as the wheel loader started to back up, the teeth on the scoop slipped off the top of the boulder, making a terrible screeching sound. Holly put her fingers in her ears. When the sound stopped, Holly continued digging in the sand at the side of the road.

We watched the wheel loader make a few more attempts to pull the boulder away.

The firefighters were taking long chains out of the ladder truck.

"I hope those chains are strong enough," Peter said.

"Are they going to put the chains around the boulder? And use the wheel loader to drag the boulder away?" Abby asked.

"Well, they're going to try that," Peter said. "But those chains don't look heavy enough."

On the first try, the chain broke.

I looked at my watch. The people had been trapped inside for more than an hour. Peter looked worried.

Suddenly Holly called out, "Know what?"

Peter smiled at her. "What?" he asked.

"I've got an idea to get the people out," Holly said. "They all have shovels, right?"

"Right." Peter seemed interested.

"They can dig a tunnel under the hill and get out that way," Holly said.

"Well," Peter said. "They actually thought of something like that, but, you see, even though the bottom of the cave is sandy, there's rock all around *outside* the cave. They would need to use explosives to get through that rock."

We were silent for a while. My watch sounded

very loud in my ears. "Tick . . . tock . . . tick . . . tock . . ."

Suddenly Holly said, "I don't like it here anymore. I want to go home. I want Mommy."

None of us said anything.

Holly repeated, "I want to go home. I want to go home," over and over.

Will went over to her. "Look," he said, "I'll help you build a really nice sand castle."

Holly shook her head. "Want to go home."

Then Abby jumped up and went over to Holly. "Holly," she said, "I'm dying to build a sand castle, too. Come on. Let's get going."

Holly looked at them. "Well, okay," she said.

I couldn't figure out why Will and Abby were so interested in making sand castles, but I was grateful that they were keeping Holly busy. I couldn't stand listening to her. You see, I wanted to go home, too. I wanted my mother.

"Your mother's doing a wonderful job," Peter whispered to me. "She keeps talking to the people inside—telling them every step that's being taken to get them out. It's important to make them feel that something is being done. Chief Mulligan wants your mother to be the only one who talks to the people inside the cave. It's more reassuring to hear the same voice."

I nodded, but I had a lump in my throat.

More police cars arrived. They were a different color. They were from the State Police. They didn't have their sirens on.

Peter stood up. "What's going on?"

I looked up and saw Sergeant Small and my mother coming toward us. My mother looked exhausted. Her face was streaked with dirt—and tears.

"What happened?" I asked. "Did he die?"

She shook her head. She seemed too tired to say anything.

"He's still holding on," Sergeant Small said, "but his breathing has become very shallow. We've radioed for more equipment, but it won't come soon enough. We've got to get him out."

"What are you going to do now?" I asked.

"A demolition squad from the State Police has just arrived. They're explosives experts. They'll probably place small charges of dynamite around the boulder."

I looked at my mother. She had a faraway look in her eyes.

"What about the person in shock?" I asked. "Won't the dynamite make him worse?"

"It's the last resort," Sergeant Small said, "but everything else has failed. We have to start clearing people out of the area."

Will, Abby, and Holly were completely absorbed in building a sand castle a few feet away from us. They didn't even look up.

"Kids sure are wonderful," I heard Sergeant Small whisper to my mother. "The way they can play even when there's a life in danger."

I looked at the sand castle. All at once I realized what Will and Abby were doing. It wasn't a sand castle at all. It was a model in sand of Thief Hill and Dragon's Mouth Cave. There was even a small rock—a miniature boulder—blocking the entrance to the cave.

Sergeant Small walked over to them and stared down at the model in the sand. He was watching Will. Will removed the little boulder and started to dig.

For a moment Sergeant Small seemed hypnotized.

My watch seemed to be very loud now. . . . "Tick . . . tock . . . tick . . . tock . . ."

"That's it!" Sergeant Small shouted. "Those kids figured it out."

He reached in the car window and called on his police radio.

"Calling Chief Mulligan," he said. There was a lot of static on the radio. Then I heard:

"Chief Mulligan here."

"It's Sergeant Small. Hold everything! We may not have to use the explosives. There may be a much easier and safer way of getting those people out . . ."

There was. Do you know how the boulder was moved? Try to figure it out . . . before you turn this page . . .

Tick . . . Tock . . . T*A*C*K

T*A*C*K's Solution:

The shock victim was moved back into the cave. Fire Chief Horton shouted instructions to Mr. Hawk. Mr. Hawk and the two other members of the team dug a big hole in the sandy bottom of the cave, but not too close to the boulder.

The wheel loader pushed the boulder into the cave—into the hole.

The hole did not have to be as big as the boulder. It just had to be deep enough to make the boulder sink down. Now there was more space between the boulder and the top of the cave. The shock victim could now be lifted over the boulder on a stretcher and taken to the hospital. (He's doing fine, by the way. My mom just called the hospital.)

The others crawled out of the cave by climbing over the top of the boulder.

I was glad to see Mr. Hawk. He once told me I had a talent for historical detective work!

Peter Barton wanted to do a news story on us and how we helped rescue the people trapped in the cave.

"Please don't," we said. "We like to keep out of the public eye."

He respected our wishes.

E–Z Parties, Inc., Makes a House Call

It has been a slow year for E–Z Parties, Incorporated.

Will and I run a small business that gives parties for little kids. We plan the parties, buy the goodies, entertain the children, and clean up afterward. For all this we charge a modest fee. Most of our clients, so far, have been the mothers of Holly's friends from school.

Since business has been bad, Will and I had a meeting at my house. We were just beginning to wonder if we should get into another business—Parties for Pets, for instance—when we got a phone call from Nicole's mother. Nicole goes to ballet school with Holly.

"Hello, dear," she said to me. "This is Tanya de Lux. Could you come right over and talk about the possibility of staging a party for my little Nicole? Her birthday is a week from this Saturday."

I told Will what she said. "Staging?" Will asked me. "That's a funny way of putting it."

"Never mind," I said. "Mrs. de Lux is an actress. She has a glamorous way of putting things. And wait till you see her house. It overlooks the water. Come on, Will, let's go! I said we'd be right over."

When we arrived, Mrs. de Lux was sitting on her terrace drinking iced tea.

"Well, aren't you two enterprising young people." She smoothed her long, black hair and smiled at us—a perfect white smile.

Then she started asking us questions. It was fun to talk about our party ideas. She seemed very interested in everything we said. Will and I were beginning to sound like experts.

"The more time we have to plan," Will said, "the better the party will be. It will also be less expensive."

I knew rich people liked to save money, so I added, "And you can save a lot of money by having Rainbow Mystery Delight instead of ice cream. Many younger children prefer it."

Mrs. de Lux leaned forward in her chair. Her beautiful green eyes sparkled.

"And *what* is Rainbow Mystery Delight?" she asked eagerly.

I told her how you put layers of orange, red, yellow, and green Jell-O in glasses. "You tilt the glasses so it looks like a rainbow."

"How clever," she said. "How charming."

". . . and it's always a good idea to have a party theme," I went on, "such as a Wild West Party, a Jungle Party, or a Circus Party."

"A Circus Party! How marvelous," Mrs. de Lux said. "Now, what sort of games do you have at a Circus Party?"

Will and I looked at each other. We had never given a Circus Party.

"Uh . . . well . . . there's Catch the Clown," I said. It sounded good. I figured I could invent the game when we got home.

"Walking a Tightrope," Will said. "Just put a clothesline on the ground. It's harder than you might imagine."

I nodded. "And then that old favorite, Spin the Lion."

The minute I said that I was sorry, but Mrs. de Lux didn't hear me. She was on her way into the house.

"Wait here a minute," she called. "There's something I must show you."

"This is going well," Will whispered.

"She's really impressed," I agreed.

Mrs. de Lux came outside with a mail-order catalog from I. M. Snowden Toys, Limited—the fanciest toy store in Winchester.

Winchester is a city about forty minutes from Sandy Harbor. Every Christmas my family makes a special trip to Winchester to see I. M. Snowden's Christmas window.

Mrs. de Lux opened the catalog to a double-page spread and showed it to me.

"I ordered this for Nicole for her birthday present," she said. "Isn't that a coincidence?"

The picture showed a miniature three-ring circus complete with a circus tent. There were small animal trainers, bareback riders, clowns, tightrope walkers, tumblers . . .

Will was leaning over my shoulder staring at the catalog.

"And the next page, too," Mrs. de Lux said. "I ordered fifty circus people and fifty animals. They're sending it by first class mail to be sure it arrives in time."

I turned the page. There were animals all over the page—lions, tigers, elephants, bears. Some of the animals were in cages.

"Each figure is made of hand-painted porcelain," the advertisement said. "Cages are separate."

I almost choked when I saw the prices.

"Do you think Nicole will like it?" Mrs. de Lux asked me.

I was about to say, *"Are you kidding?"* but I caught myself in time and said, "I think it would be a suitable gift for a child of that age, and it does fit in rather well with a Circus Party theme."

When we got back to my house, we were very excited. We were sure we had gotten the job.

"We shouldn't say a word to anyone yet," Will said. "Not until we get the job for sure. Not until she calls us."

Unfortunately, my little sister Holly overheard us talking. Before we knew it, she had told everyone in the world we were putting on Nicole's birthday party.

Two days went by. We didn't hear from Mrs. de Lux, but we went right ahead with plans for the party. We thought up lots of circus games and put them in a card file.

We made up a terrific circus skit with costumes and everything. We really worked hard.

On Friday Will said, "There's only a week until the party. I hope she calls us today. Otherwise we'll have to do all the shopping and decorating at the last minute."

On Monday I said, "Maybe she lost our number."

"She could always look it up in the phone book," Will said. "I just don't understand it."

It was getting embarrassing to explain to people that we still hadn't heard about the job.

The Tuesday before the party, Holly got an invitation in the mail from Nicole:

COME TO MY CIRCUS PARTY
Saturday at 3 P.M.
Starring a Fabulous Mystery Dessert!

I grabbed the invitation and ran over to Will's house.

"Look at this!" I said. I snapped the invitation open. I was so angry I almost ripped it in two.

"Do you realize that all she was doing was picking our brains?" Will asked me. He was furious.

"She didn't even call us. Then she goes and steals our ideas," I added. "I hope this turns out to be one of the worst parties of all time."

On Saturday, the day of Nicole's party, Will and I were once again discussing our new business venture—Parties for Pets.

We had just decided that although cat and dog birthday parties might be fun, parakeet parties might prove a little disappointing.

At noon the telephone rang. I almost didn't recognize Mrs. de Lux's voice. She sounded so childlike.

"Oh, dear," she kept saying helplessly. "What am I going to do?"

"Is something the matter?" I asked politely. I was grinning from ear to ear.

"Everything went wrong," she said. "I ruined everything. And I spent all night in the library looking up those circus games you mentioned, but I couldn't find them anyplace."

"Most of those games come from Persia," I said. "You have to be able to read the language." (I felt quite wicked.)

"Oh, I knew I should have hired you two," Mrs. de Lux wailed.

I waited. I didn't say a word.

"Oh, please come and see if there's anything you can do," she begged me.

"You told her we would come?" Will couldn't get over it. "Why didn't you just say we don't make last-minute house calls?"

"Oh, well," I said. "E–Z Parties needs the business. If we do a good job, word will get around, and one job leads to another. Besides, I want to see how much she's messed up."

Nicole answered the door. We stood there with our card file of circus games and all our costumes for the skit.

"Will my party be all right?" she asked us anxiously.

"Of course," I said.

"Mommy's in the kitchen. She's waiting for you. I'm not allowed to go in," Nicole told us.

Will knocked on the kitchen door. "E–Z Parties has arrived," he announced.

Mrs. de Lux opened the door a crack. She let us in. She looked just awful. There were big rings under her eyes. She wasn't wearing any makeup.

"Thank goodness you're here," she said. "Just look at those Rainbow Mystery Delights. I did exactly what you said, but they just don't look right."

On the counter was a tray of plastic glasses. Inside each glass was a brownish-red pudding.

"Excuse me," I said, "but did you let each color of Jell-O set separately before you put on the next layer?"

"Why would I do that?" she asked. "I just poured them in on top of each other."

Will and I looked at each other. We knew it was too late to do anything.

"It's a nice earthy color," I said. "And it probably tastes just fine."

"That's the ugliest dessert I've ever seen," Mrs. de Lux said.

". . . and it fits the invitation," I went on. "It certainly is a Mystery Dessert."

"I've got to have a Mystery Dessert," Mrs. de Lux said. "Ice cream won't do."

Will studied the murky pudding.

"I've got an idea," he said. "Do you have a small pair of scissors?"

We watched as Will took one plastic glass of Jell-O and turned it upside down on a plate. Carefully he cut the plastic glass off with the scissors. The Jell-O was very hard.

"It's all in the name," Will said. "Children are very impressed with names. Now, do you have a birthday candle and holder?"

Mrs. de Lux brought them to him. Will stuck the candle in the middle of the cone-shaped mound. He lit the candle.

"VOLCANO SURPRISE!" he said.

It looked very impressive. I thought a whole tray of them would be quite dramatic.

"That's wonderful," Mrs. de Lux said. "Now, we'll have the party on the terrace; you have the games . . ."

". . . and a ten-minute skit," I said.

"Do you think we need any decorations?" she asked.

Will and I stared at her in disbelief. A Circus Party without decorations! And it was already 1 P.M.!

My heart sank. Up until that point, I had really believed that E–Z Parties, Inc., could save Nicole's party.

"We usually recommend decorations," Will murmured, "especially at a Circus Party."

"Maybe I have some balloons around." Mrs. de Lux searched around in a cabinet. She pulled out a small, open package of balloons.

"Left over from last year," Mrs. de Lux said. "We can decorate the terrace with them. Won't that be festive?"

Will and I looked at each other. There were about six balloons in that package.

"Well, you won't have a cluttered look," I said. Then I noticed a large package in the corner of the kitchen. It was covered in brown wrapping paper. FIRST CLASS MAIL was stamped all over it.

"By any chance, is that the circus kit from I. M. Snowden?" I asked Mrs. de Lux.

"Why, yes, it is," Mrs. de Lux said. "I haven't opened it yet. I thought we'd wait for the party to begin. Nicole likes to share her toys with her friends. It is more fun for her that way."

Will and I got the idea at the same time.

"Why don't we open it now?" Will asked. "We could set it up on the glass table on the terrace."

"It could be a birthday surprise for Nicole and decorations for a Circus Party at the same time," I said.

"A main exhibit," Will explained.

"A centerpiece." I was really excited now. "We'll put the balloons around the table. Simple but elegant!"

Mrs. de Lux took a deep breath and smiled. "I just want you to know that I think E–Z Parties is a lifesaver."

"Why don't you just go upstairs and get dressed," I said kindly. "Let Nicole blow up the balloons. That way she can stay in her room while we get ready."

Will and I carried the big package to the terrace. Carefully we took off the brown wrapping paper and opened the box. I was thrilled to be opening a package from I. M. Snowden Toys, Limited.

Everything was wrapped in lots of packing paper. We assembled the three-ring circus first. Then we set up the blue-and-white circus tent around it and lifted the flaps. We hung the trapezes inside. The directions that came with the circus kit were very clear.

It looked beautiful.

Then we took out the little circus people and placed them carefully around the ring.

"Look at those clowns!" I breathed. "Each one is different."

I looked at Will. He was feeling around in the box, searching through the packing papers.

"The animals aren't here," he said. He took out the green packing slip. "Toria," he said slowly. "It says that the animals are supposed to be in the box—fifty animals!"

But there weren't any animals at all.

"What's a circus without animals?" I groaned.

I went to the foot of the stairs and called up to Mrs. de Lux. A minute later she came down. She was wearing a beautiful blue silk dress and makeup.

"You look very nice," I whispered. "But the animals aren't here."

"Of course not," Mrs. de Lux whispered back. "They're not invited to come until three o'clock. It's only one-thirty now."

I stared at her. Then I realized what she thought I had meant. "Not the children," I said. "The animals. The circus animals. They're not in the box!"

"But they have to be," she gasped. "I paid a fortune for them. Fifty animals."

She came out to the terrace and searched through the box. Then she went straight to the telephone in the kitchen. We stood there as she

dialed long-distance and asked to talk to someone in the mail-order department at I. M.
Snowden.

We listened as she explained about the package and the party. "The circus animals are
missing, and they're the most important part.
My daughter's party begins in less than an
hour and a half."

She put her hand over the mouthpiece and
said to us, "She's gone to check our order. She's
very nice, and it's a very reliable store. This
woman says that if by any chance the firm of
I. M. Snowden has made a mistake, they will
send the animals right out to us by special
messenger. They will be here in time for the
party."

"Well, of course they made a mistake," I said.
"The animals aren't here."

"Hello?" The woman at the other end of the
phone was back. We watched Mrs. de Lux's
face as she listened.

"But the animals *aren't* here," Mrs de Lux
wailed. "They're simply not in the box. How
dare you suggest such a thing! Hold on a minute," she told the woman.

She covered the mouthpiece again. "Their

records show that the animals were packed in the box. In a very polite way, of course, this woman is suggesting that I am lying—that the animals are really here. They'll only send the special truck out if we can *prove* those animals weren't in the box."

"Well, just tell them you have two eye-witnesses right here who will swear there were no animals in the box," I said. I looked around. Will had left the kitchen.

"Good point," Mrs. de Lux said to me and told the woman she had two eyewitnesses who were no relation to her. "So they have no reason to lie," she said.

But that wasn't good enough.

"How in the world could we ever give you *definite* proof?" Mrs. de Lux was very upset now. "Do you really think I would hide those animals in my house and say they never came?"

Will suddenly appeared in the kitchen again. He was carrying the brown wrapping paper under his arm.

"Don't hang up. We *do* have definite proof that those animals were never sent in that box," he told Mrs. de Lux. "And there is still time for I. M. Snowden to send a special messenger to get here before Nicole's party. Let me talk to her . . . "

Mrs. de Lux handed Will the phone.

By the time Will hung up, the animals were being packed and on their way to Sandy Harbor. Do you know what Will said? Do you know how Will proved those animals were not in that box?

E–Z Parties, Inc., Makes a House Call

Will's Solution:

The circus animals arrived in time and we set them up. Nicole and her friends just loved it!

The people from I. M. Snowden Toys, Limited, were very apologetic.

They realized, as soon as Will told them, that the proof was in the amount of postage. Since the package was sent by first class mail, the amount of the postage showed how much the package weighed. If the package had had the fifty circus animals inside, it would have been heavier. It would have needed more postage.

Mrs. de Lux had the outer wrapping to prove there was not enough postage!

The party went beautifully. The children liked our little circus skit so much we had to do it over and over. Holly was very proud.

To our surprise, E–Z Parties, Inc., got double our usual fee from Tanya de Lux.

"For performance beyond the call of duty," she said.

T*A*C*K Covers the Waterfront

This morning Will, Chuck, and I went down to the boat docks to see if we could find Johnny Engels. We were hoping he could take us out on his sailboat, the *Sea Rat*. Johnny is the best sailor in Sandy Harbor. He is teaching us to sail.

The *Sea Rat* was tied up at the dock. The cover was on the boat. Johnny wasn't around.

"There's Mr. Morash," Will said. "Let's go ask him if he knows where Johnny is."

Mr. Morash rents out small rowboats in the harbor. He was standing down on the beach, puffing on his pipe and watching an artist at work on a painting.

Artists like to come to Sandy Harbor in the summertime. It is very picturesque. There are motorboats, fishing boats, and white sails all over the harbor. A small ferry runs once an hour from Sandy Harbor to the far end of Corkhill Island across the bay. Very often the artists sell their paintings right off their easels to the tourists.

Most artists we see look like ordinary people, but the man Mr. Morash was watching really looked like an artist. He was wearing a black beret and a blue smock. He had an enormous red beard and small, thick glasses.

"Maybe he's famous," Chuck whispered as we got closer.

Just then the artist stood up and walked over to the edge of the water. He stood on a rock with his hand on his hip and peered intently down at the waves lapping against the shore. He didn't move for a whole minute. He seemed to be studying each wave. Then he went back to his easel.

I was very impressed.

Mr. Morash saw us and came over.

"Interesting fellow," he said to us. "Name of Thornton Witticut. Been here a week. Lives on that old cabin cruiser tied up at the end of the pier. Don't know much about art myself, but I like to watch these creative fellows work."

"We were looking for Johnny Engels," Will said. "Have you seen him around?"

"Johnny went out with his father to check the salmon nets. Should have been back by now." Mr. Morash looked at his watch. "Why don't you go wait for him over on Eddie's wharf?"

Johnny's father, Eddie Engels, is a fisherman. He owns a small, thirty-foot fishing boat. His fishing shed and docks are right around the cove from the boat dock.

"Hope there's no trouble," Mr. Morash said. "But I wouldn't be the least bit surprised if there was—the way Eddie Engels has been acting lately. Not the least bit surprised." He shook his head sadly and went back to watch the artist with the beard.

"What did he mean by that?" I asked Will as we walked along the shore road to the fishing wharves.

"I'm not sure," Will said. "But I think it has to do with that Fiske Fish Company."

"Are they the ones who own those big refrigerated trucks—the trucks that come around and pick up the fish from the fishermen?" Chuck asked.

Will nodded. "I heard Mr. Engels talking to

my dad at the hardware store. Two weeks ago, Fiske doubled their prices for taking the fish into market. Mr. Engels got mad and went out and bought his own truck."

"That sounds like a good idea," I said. "Why should he get into trouble?"

"Well, the Fiske Fish Company doesn't like Eddie Engels trucking his own fish into market. They're afraid other fishermen will start doing the same thing," Will told us.

"Why don't they?" I asked. "It sounds like a good idea."

"It is," Will said, "and in the end it would be much cheaper. Mr. Engels even told the other Sandy Harbor fishermen he would take their fish in, too. All they would have to do is help pay for running the truck."

"Are they going to do it?" Chuck asked.

"They're thinking about it," Will said, "but some of them are scared. There are some tough characters who work for Fiske. Mr. Engels told Dad he got a threatening phone call the day he bought the truck."

Eddie Engels' garage is right next to his fish shed. When we passed it, we peeked in at his new truck. It was very big.

Then we walked around the fish shed and

went down to the wharf to wait for Johnny.

We didn't have long to wait. We could see Mr. Engels' fishing boat coming across the water. It was piled high with nets.

"I don't get it," Will said. "I thought they just went out to check the nets. What are they bringing them in for?"

As the boat pulled into the dock, Johnny waved to us. Mr. Engels climbed out and tied a line to the dock. He didn't say anything to us, but he's not much of a talker anyway. He turned to Johnny and mumbled, "Help me get these nets out."

We stood silently and watched as Johnny and his father collected the nets and brought them up on the wharf.

"What happened?" I finally asked.

Johnny picked up part of one net and showed us. "Our nets were cut," he said. "All slashed up. Someone did it during the night."

"Looks like we have some work to do," Will said as we walked back toward the boat dock.

"Right." Chuck was furious. "Find out who slashed Eddie Engels' nets."

"Well, if we hang around the docks we're bound to notice something," I said. "We'll just have to keep our eyes and ears open—the way detectives do in movies."

"T*A*C*K covers the waterfront," Will said.

"Exactly," I said, "and we'll act like we're just kids hanging around. No one pays much attention to kids."

"We *are* kids," Chuck said.

"All the better," I said. "That will make our disguise more realistic."

SANDY HARBOR, WEDNESDAY, JULY 22—

We were down at the docks bright and early. We heard Mr. Morash talking to one of the fishermen. He said that Johnny and his father had spent most of the night repairing the nets.

"Early this morning they were ready to go out and set those nets again," we heard Mr. Morash say, "and Eddie couldn't get his engine going. Ran his battery flat trying to start it. Turned out someone had put water in his gasoline tank."

"Same person as slashed those nets, more than likely," the fisherman said. "Gotta be someone from that Fiske Company, but the Coast Guard can't do a thing unless they catch 'em in the act."

Mr. Morash puffed on his pipe thoughtfully. "You know, if Eddie were smart, he'd get into another line of work. Open a little gift shop or something like that."

"He'd never do that," the fisherman said. "Not Eddie Engels. He's been fishing around here his whole life. His father and grandfather were both fishermen. I know how he feels. Most of us are the same way."

We spent the morning snooping around. Every time the ferry from Corkhill Island came into the dock, we studied the people getting on and off.

I walked around writing down the license plates of suspicious-looking cars parked around the waterfront.

"What makes a car look suspicious, Toria?" Chuck asked me.

"I don't know, Chuck," I said. "I just get a kind of feeling about some of them—the way they're parked . . ."

". . . the sneaky look in their headlights," Will added.

"What else can we do?" I was feeling discouraged. "We've been here all day and we haven't seen a single thug. Just lots of nice, friendly tourists and summer people from Corkhill."

We passed the artist with the red beard sitting by the side of the road near the fishing wharves. He was talking to a couple who were standing behind him watching him paint.

"You see, my work is in the primitive school of painting," the artist was saying in a very refined voice. "The beauty of nature to the untrained eye. Now, what I am searching for is a certain tension between sky and water, land and sea, wave and rock . . ."

We went over to take a look at the painting. I couldn't believe my eyes. It was the worst painting I have ever seen. The boats didn't even look as if they were in the water. The sea had lumps all over it, which I suppose were supposed to be waves. The painting must have been finished because the artist had signed his name in large, neat handwriting: *Thornton Witticut*. That was the best part.

"That's the most pitiful painting I've ever seen," I said after we had quietly moved away.

"Well, at least he's getting a good sunburn," Chuck said. "With that red beard he's beginning to look like a lobster."

"A lobster could do a better painting," Will said, "with his claws tied behind his back."

There were thunderstorms all day today. Will had to work in his father's store, and Chuck had to help his mother move furniture around the living room. We couldn't do a thing.

More thunderstorms! I finally decided that I would go down to the docks anyway to do some private investigating.

I was almost out the door when my mother caught me. "Toria," she said, "you're not going out—especially in that ratty old trench coat. Put it back in the attic where you found it."

At six o'clock this evening, Will called.

"Eddie Engels was just in the hardware store," he said. "Someone unplugged that big freezer in his fishing shed. All his bait is rotten. He says it must have been unplugged during the day on Wednesday."

"But we were around all day!" I said.

"He had a week's worth of bait in that freezer." Will lowered his voice. "Toria, it's sabotage. They're trying to drive Eddie Engels out of business. He said he felt like giving up!"

SATURDAY, JULY 25—

When we got down to the boat dock this morning, we saw Johnny on the deck of the *Sea Rat,* raising his sails!

Johnny saw us and called, "Come on. What are you waiting for? I wasn't planning to sail this boat by myself."

We watched in amazement as Johnny straightened out some lines on the deck. He was whistling.

"The police caught 'em, right?" I said.

"Nope," Johnny said, and went on whistling.

"Well, then, how come you're so cheerful?" Chuck asked him.

"Hop in and I'll tell you," Johnny said.

We all climbed into the *Sea Rat* and sat down.

"You see," Johnny began, "last night the fishermen around here had a meeting. They were really angry at what's been going on. They are sure Fiske is sabotaging Dad's business. At the end they decided they were going to all ship their fish to market in my father's truck. They're even going to pay him something. The Sandy Harbor fishermen are refusing to use the Fiske Fish Company!"

"You mean they're all sticking together?" Will asked.

"Yup," Johnny said. "And they got the Coast Guard to put more patrol boats out at night to keep an eye on the nets." Johnny smiled at us. "Well, that's enough of that. Just look at this day. It's perfect sailing weather. Why don't we use the spinnaker? It's up in the fishing shed."

The spinnaker is an enormous sail that billows out in front of a sailboat. It looks like a parachute. Johnny's spinnaker is bright orange and white. It's very exciting to sail with a spinnaker.

Chuck and I ran up to get it while Johnny and Will got the boat ready.

I followed Chuck around the garage next to

the shed. When Chuck passed the side door, he stumbled on an easel leaning up against the garage. Next to the easel was Mr. Witticut's large canvas bag with a painting on top of it. It was even worse than the one we had seen the other day.

Chuck came to sudden stop. He turned and looked into the window of the garage.

"Toria," he whispered, "come here. Mr. Engels' truck looks funny. It's kneeling."

I peered in the window of the garage.

"The front tires are flat," I said. "That's why it looks funny."

I put my hands around my eyes so I could see better.

" . . . and I'll tell you what looks even funnier," I said to Chuck in a flat voice.

"What?" he asked.

"Mr. Witticut slashing tires with a great big knife."

"We've got to stop him!" Chuck said.

I grabbed Chuck and held onto him with all my might. I pulled him down under the window.

"Chuck," I whispered. "I do not think that would be advisable. You may have noticed the size of that knife. It is quite a large knife. It is probably quite sharp." (I always seem to talk in this careful way when I am scared to death.)

Chuck nodded.

"We'll follow him, then," he whispered.

"At a distance," I whispered back.

We crept back along the side of the garage.

When we came to the side door, it flew open. We were standing face to face with Mr. Witticut.

"I thought I heard something." Mr. Witticut spoke in a quiet voice, but he was still clutching the knife.

Chuck turned to run and tripped over the easel. I tripped over Chuck. The oil painting landed on my lap. It was still wet.

"If you'll be kind enough to move aside," Mr. Witticut said in his refined voice. He reached over me, grabbed his canvas bag, and took off down the shore road toward the docks.

"Let's go!" Chuck scrambled to his feet. "He's going to get away."

"Not too close!" I screamed after Chuck.

Mr. Witticut was a fast runner. He quickly disappeared around the bend where the road follows the cove.

"Slow down!" I screamed to Chuck. "He might be hiding. He might jump out at you."

Chuck disappeared around the bend, too.

I lost sight of both of them.

When I finally caught up to Chuck, he was standing on the boat dock staring at the old cabin cruiser tied up at the end. He was shaking his head.

"I don't believe it," he said. "I was sure he was heading toward his boat. I was sure that's how he was going to try to get away."

Will and Johnny were running toward us. When we told them what had happened, Johnny said, "I just saw Witticut get on the ferry, and the ferry's leaving right this minute!"

I turned and looked. The Corkhill Ferry was pulling away from the dock.

"We're calling the Coast Guard," Johnny said.

We followed Johnny to a large sailboat tied up next to the *Sea Rat.* A woman with a scarf around her head was painting the deck.

"Can we use your marine radio?" Johnny asked her. "It's an emergency."

The woman looked up. "What's wrong?" she asked. Then she saw our faces. "Of course you may. Go right ahead!"

We went down into the cabin of the sailboat, which was named *Kon Tiki.* Johnny went to the marine radio and called the Coast Guard.

A few seconds later we heard: "Sandy Harbor Coast Guard. Go ahead, *Kon Tiki.*"

Johnny quickly gave them the information. He told them the man was on the ferry and the ferry had just pulled out.

"Stand by," said the voice on the marine radio. Then he said, "We're sending a boat right away to the ferry dock over at Corkhill. We'll stop the ferry at the other end and look for the man. Please repeat your description."

Johnny said, "Thick red beard, small rimless eyeglasses, black beret, blue smock, brown corduroy pants, and sandals. Oh, yes, he has a large canvas bag that might contain a knife."

"Thank you. Listen carefully. This is Petty Officer Crew. We want you to stay right by that radio until we get back to you."

Fifteen minutes went by. Twenty minutes. Then half an hour . . .

It was an hour and a half before we heard.

"Calling the sailboat *Kon Tiki*. This is the Sandy Harbor Coast Guard, Petty Officer Crew. One of our officers boarded the Corkhill Ferry over an hour ago. He is still holding all the passengers on board. I'm afraid there is no one who fits your description."

"No one with a red beard?" Johnny asked.

"No one with a red beard," Petty Officer Crew reported. "And there are at least one hundred passengers on board."

"Maybe he jumped overboard," I whispered.

"No," Will said. "It's too dangerous. I think it's more likely that that beard was a fake."

"But it looked so real," Chuck said.

The radio crackled. Then we heard Petty Officer Crew say, "Stand by, *Kon Tiki* . . ."

We waited. After a few seconds he said, "They just finished searching the ship. We received a message from the officer on board the ferry. He said they found a canvas bag floating alongside the ferry. The clothes you described are in it. There's also a large knife and a red beard."

"Then he's still on the ferry," Johnny said.

"He must be," Petty Officer Crew said. "No one's been allowed to get off. But do you think you could identify this man *without* his beard? If not, we'll have to let everybody go. We can't hold the passengers much longer. And the ferry has to make its return run."

Johnny turned to us. "It seems to me that without the beard and eyeglasses, it would be impossible. He always wore that beret so we don't even know what color hair he has. We wouldn't have the faintest idea what that Thornton Witticut really looks like."

"No," Will said. "We wouldn't. But we can pick him out in no time."

"How can we pick him out if we don't know what he looks like, Will?" I asked. "You're not making any sense."

But the Coast Guard thought Will was making sense when he told them how to identify Mr. Witticut. Do you know what he said?

T*A*C*K Covers the Waterfront

Will's Solution:

Mr. Thornton Witticut was picked out from the other passengers immediately.

As it turned out, his real name is Otto Fiske, the younger brother of Stanley Fiske, owner of Fiske Fish Company. Otto Fiske really is an artist (at least he thinks so), but since he doesn't sell too many paintings, he does sabotage on the side for his brother.

The slashed tires on Mr. Engels' truck were replaced right away, and it was ready to roll on Monday. The Coast Guard and Fisheries Board are now conducting an investigation of the Fiske Fish Company.

You see, there was only one man on that ferry whose face was two different shades: bright red where he got the sunburn and very pale where the fake beard had been covering his face!

Duchess on Trial

Will and I haven't seen Chuck for a whole week. We both talked to him on the phone. He sounded very unhappy. All he would say was that his mother's decorator was driving him crazy.

Now that Chuck's puppy, Duchess, has stopped chewing up furniture, Chuck's mother has been redecorating her whole house. She hired Vera Hopewell, the fanciest decorator in town, to do it. Everyone says the decorator has gotten Elisabeth Finney (Chuck's mother) to spend a fortune.

We decided to drop in on Chuck and find out what was going on.

On the way to Chuck's house, we stopped at

the post office. T*A*C*K has a post office box. We each use part of our allowance each month to pay for it. There was a letter in our box.

I looked at the envelope. It was from Abby.

"Let's not open it yet," I said. "Let's save it for Chuck. A letter from Abby will cheer him up."

There was a large truck that said PEERLESS PAINTERS parked in front of Chuck's house. There was also a strange car in the driveway.

When we pushed the doorbell, we heard chimes ringing inside the house.

"That's new," I said to Will.

The door was opened by Vera Hopewell, the decorator. She seemed a little distracted.

"Oh," she said. "You must be Chucky's friends. He's upstairs. I'm terribly involved right now putting the finishing touches on this foyer. Elisabeth went to the airport to pick up Bruce. He's been away on a case. We're going to surprise him."

Chuck's father, Bruce Finney, is a lawyer. He often goes away on big law cases. I felt a little uncomfortable. Mrs. Hopewell talked as if she were a part of the family.

When I saw the foyer, I felt even more uncomfortable. It looked like a room in a museum. I thought there should be one of those thick, red velvet ropes across the foyer to keep the public out.

The floor had been done in black-and-white marble squares. The wall was covered with ivory satin wallpaper and there was a crystal chandelier hanging from the ceiling. Against one wall stood a white marble table with a tall, brass candlestick on it. There were stiff, wooden chairs on either side. Each chair had a light blue satin cushion on the seat. Above the table was one of the most beautiful mirrors I have ever seen. It had a gold frame around it.

"I simply can't wait for Elisabeth to see this mirror," Mrs. Hopewell said. "It just arrived. Magnificent piece—over eighty years old." She tilted her head to one side. "I'm not sure that mirror is straight."

Mrs. Hopewell went over to adjust the mirror. Will and I crept up the stairs.

We could hear Duchess whimpering in the kitchen.

Duchess is one of the cutest puppies I have ever known. She is white and shaggy. It is terrible to hear her cry.

"This doesn't seem too hopeful," Will whispered. "Everything looks so *perfect!*"

When we got upstairs, Chuck's door was closed.

"Look at that door," Will said. He gasped.

The door to Chuck's room was painted an electric blue with silver stars on it. In big silver and red letters, it said:

We knocked.

Chuck opened the door. Will and I stepped into his room. The next thing we knew, Chuck was pushing us out the door, yelling, "No, no! I don't want you to see it." He slammed the door in our faces.

But it was too late. We'd already seen the batmobile bed and the flying saucer lampshades . . .

A second later Chuck came out into the hall. He closed the door behind him.

"I'm sorry I did that," he said. "But it's so embarrassing."

"Did Mrs. Hopewell decorate your room?" Will asked.

Chuck nodded unhappily.

"I guess she painted that stuff on your door," I said. I felt very sorry for Chuck.

"She got an artist to do it," Chuck said. "Mrs. Hopewell says children like bright colors."

"Yes," I said. "I noticed your walls, but how come one wall is all black?"

"So I can stare at it and use my imagination," Chuck mumbled. "She calls it my Imagination Screen."

"How awful," I said.

"But that's not the worst part," Chuck said.

"What's the worst part?" Will asked him.

"Mrs. Hopewell is trying to get Mom to get rid of Duchess. Every time a new antique lamp or something arrives, she says, 'Elisabeth, you're not really going to keep that animal, are you?' "

Will and I didn't know what to say.

"And when the Chinese rug arrived yesterday for Dad's study, Mrs. Hopewell said, 'That puppy's going to grow up to be a monster. Just look at those enormous feet!' "

Chuck refused to go back into his room to talk. "We can't go into the backyard either," he said. "The painters are painting the patio."

"We could keep Duchess company in the kitchen," I suggested. Then I remembered Abby's letter. "And we have something to show you that will certainly cheer you up."

When we passed the foyer, Mrs. Hopewell was still trying to get the mirror straight.

Duchess was glad to see us. She wiggled her whole body around, but when we sat down at the table, she curled up under it and lay there with her chin on her paws.

"She's depressed," Chuck explained. "And when Duchess is depressed, I'm depressed."

I took out Abby's letter and handed it to Chuck. "We saved it for you to open."

Chuck opened the letter and read it. Then he put it on the table and stared out the back window at the painters who were slapping white paint on the patio.

I picked up the letter. It was written in the tiniest handwriting. Abby only writes like that when she's unhappy.

Dear T*A*C*K:

I just can't believe what's happening. Mom and Dad just told me we're moving again. We're moving to the outskirts of Pleasantville—to the middle of nowhere. Dad went and bought a sheep farm a mile from Pleasant Peak.

At the time my parents did not say, "Abby, how do you feel about sheep?" They did not say, "We won't move unless *you* feel comfortable about it." I was not consulted at all!

I will still go to the same school, but now I have to spend two hours every day on the school bus. And you should see the kids who ride that bus!

I've never felt so lonely. What am I going to do?

Your Friend in Misery,

Abby.

We now had two miserable friends. One half of the T*A*C*K team was down in the dumps. I showed the letter to Will.

"We can't tell her to run away from home," I said. "I don't see what T*A*C*K can do."

"Let's write to her," Will said. "At least she'll feel less lonely. Do you have some paper?" he asked Chuck.

Chuck nodded and pointed to a pad on the kitchen counter. Then I saw him take his wallet out of his pocket. He took a photo out of the wallet and stared blankly at it. It was a color photo of Duchess—Duchess in happier days.

All at once we heard a crash.

"Duchess!" Chuck yelled and jumped to his feet. "She's knocked something over!"

"Chuck," I said. "Calm down. Duchess is right under the table—right under your feet."

"Oh," Chuck said, but he still seemed nervous.

"Everything's perfectly all right!" Mrs. Hopewell called from the foyer. "The mirror just slipped, but luckily it landed right on the table. Just stay where you are. Everything is perfectly fine."

We started to work on the letter to Abby. We didn't get very far.

"Chucky!" Mrs. Hopewell called in a high-pitched voice. "Chucky, go pick me a big bunch of flowers immediately."

We went to the foyer. Mrs. Hopewell was placing a large vase on the marble table across from the brass candlestick.

"Don't just stand there, children," she said crossly. *"Move!"*

"That's not her usual way of talking," Chuck

whispered as we went out into Mrs. Finney's garden to pick some flowers.

When we had gathered a big bunch of flowers, I carried them into the foyer.

Mrs. Hopewell grabbed them out of my arms and stuck them into the vase. She did not even arrange them. She had a funny look on her face. Then she picked up her pocketbook, slung it over her shoulder, and left the house.

We stared after her as she jumped into her car, which took off like a batmobile.

"Weird," Chuck said.

I was looking at the vase. "I liked the table better without the vase," I said, "and there isn't even any water in it. She forgot to put water in the vase."

Then I noticed something else. "Hey! There's a crack in the mirror. Right behind the vase!"

It looked like this:

"I'll bet it happened when she dropped the mirror on the table," I said. "It had to. And she put the vase there to hide the crack!"

Just then we heard a car pull into the driveway.

"It's Mom and Dad," Chuck said. "We'd better go out there and tell Mom what happened. I never trusted that Mrs. Hopewell."

When we got outside, Mrs. Finney was standing on the lawn tying a blindfold over her husband's eyes.

"This is ridiculous, Elisabeth," Bruce Finney said. He was wearing a three-piece suit and carrying a leather briefcase.

"Oh, come on, dear," Mrs. Finney said. "I want this to be a big surprise."

"Mom, I have something to tell you," Chuck began.

"Not now, dear," his mother said. "Don't spoil this moment, please."

"But Mom, please listen," Chuck said.

"Sh-h-h, Chuck. Take your father's briefcase and carry it for him." Mrs. Finney's face was all flushed.

Chuck did what he was told.

As we walked into the house, I was glad for a moment that the big vase was covering the crack in the mirror. Then I saw that something else was covering the mirror, too.

Sitting in the middle of the white marble table, between the candlestick and the vase, was a shaggy, white puppy. Duchess was looking at herself in the new mirror.

Chuck's mother screamed. She screamed again.

His father ripped the blindfold off his eyes. "What's wrong?" he yelled.

"Get out!" Mrs. Finney shrieked at Duchess.

Duchess took one last look at herself in the mirror and jumped off the table onto a chair.

As she jumped, she knocked over the brass candlestick which fell against the mirror. To my horror, there was now a big, spidery-looking crack in the mirror—a second crack!

Duchess disappeared out the front door.

No one spoke for a while. Then Mrs. Finney said in a dull voice, "Duchess broke the mirror. That's the end. Vera was right. We're getting rid of that dog."

Chuck lost his temper. "But, Mom, I've been trying to tell you. . . . Mrs. Hopewell already broke the mirror. She broke it first. She dropped it."

Chuck's mother stared at him. "Are you completely crazy, Chuck? We were all standing here when Duchess did it."

"Look," Chuck said. "Behind the vase." He started to move the vase.

"Don't touch that vase," Chuck's mother said sharply. "That'll be broken, too."

It was Mr. Finney who moved the vase and stuck it on the floor. "This room looks like a funeral parlor," I heard him mutter.

"Now you see," Chuck said. "There are two cracks."

But there weren't two cracks. The crack in

the corner and the spidery crack had run together.

"One enormous crack," Mrs. Finney said. "And Duchess is responsible."

"Vera Hopewell is responsible," Chuck said. "The mirror was already cracked before you got here."

"Vera Hopewell is one of the most careful people I know," Mrs. Finney said in a cold voice. "We're not discussing this any further. Duchess goes!"

Chuck stood there speechless.

"Wait a minute," Will said. He turned to Mr. Finney. "Mr. Finney, isn't it true that *legally*, if the mirror had already been broken, it can't be broken again?"

"What are you talking about, Will Roberts?" Chuck's mother said.

"Actually, Elisabeth," Mr. Finney said, "Will has a point. If, by any chance, Mrs. Hopewell dropped that mirror and cracked it *before* Duchess cracked it, she is to blame. Of course it would have to be proven that there are two cracks and that one was made before the other."

He sat down on one of the wooden chairs.

"It's a very interesting point of law," he said. "There's a famous case . . . "

"Don't sit on that chair, Bruce!" Mrs. Finney said angrily. "Those chairs are not meant for sitting on."

"Well, then, we'll take the discussion into my study, Elisabeth," Bruce Finney said. "Unless you did something with my favorite furniture."

"I didn't touch that battered, old stuff, Bruce, but the new Chinese rug has been laid down, so the children must remove their shoes." Mrs. Finney looked very unhappy.

Before we left the foyer, Will went into the kitchen and got the pad of paper. Very carefully he copied the pattern of the cracks in the mirror. It looked like this:

Then we all went into Mr. Finney's study. Chuck, Will, and I sat on a comfortable, brown couch. I looked around at the bookcases that were filled with law books. The Chinese rug was quite beautiful, with large gold and blue designs on a brown background.

Mrs. Finney sat on an armchair with her back to the door, and Mr. Finney sat at his desk.

"As I was saying, there's a famous case—a murder case in which it was decided that a person couldn't be charged with the murder because the person he killed was already dead. It actually happened . . . "

I liked listening to Mr. Finney's calm, reasonable voice. I was sure he must be an excellent lawyer. I also liked sitting in the study with bookcases from floor to ceiling. It seemed to me that in this room justice would be done.

Then I noticed that Duchess was standing in the doorway behind Mrs. Finney's chair. She was sitting quietly. She seemed to be listening. She had come to her own trial. Like a good defendant, she looked very innocent. Even her paws seemed unusually clean.

"But a murder is intentional," Will said. "It's a criminal case. This was an accident."

(Duchess walked across the room and sat in front of Will. She seemed to know Will was defending her—that he was going to clear her of the charge.)

"Even in a case like this," Mr. Finney said, "where the wrong done is accidental, the first party is responsible—unless, of course, the two parties were working together. Then both parties are guilty."

"Bruce," Mrs. Finney said, "it's highly unlikely that Duchess and Mrs. Hopewell were working together, and if you ask me . . . "

"Correct. They were not working together," Mr. Finney said. "Now, if it can be proven that there was already a crack in the mirror before Duchess knocked over the candlestick . . . "

"Wait a minute," Will said. "I think I can prove it. Just give me a few seconds."

He was staring at the pad of paper with the picture of the crack. I peeked over his shoulder. Then, all at once, I knew Will could prove that the crack in the corner had been there first.

As I waited for Will's answer, I looked down at the Chinese rug. I got a funny sensation. It was as if the pattern of the rug had changed before my eyes. There were more white spots in the rug than I remembered. The pattern of each spot was in the shape of a pawprint—Duchess's pawprint. Duchess had white paint from the patio all over her paws. That's why they looked so clean.

Do you know how we proved there was already a crack in the mirror? Guess if you really want to . . . not that it matters anymore, because now Duchess is in big trouble!

Duchess on Trial

Will and Toria's Solution:

Dear Abby:

We are afraid this letter will be pretty depressing. We cannot help you with your misery right now. You see, Chuck's mother is getting rid of Duchess. He has one week to find her a new home; after that Duchess goes to the Animal Shelter. It's a long story, but unfortunately white paint that is used to paint a patio is very hard to remove from an expensive Chinese rug.

Yesterday we won a case to save Duchess (before the pawprints were noticed). It all had to do with a cracked mirror. Will and I were quite brilliant. Bruce Finney was very impressed with our logic. We won on the grounds that a crack made earlier will stop the spread of a crack made later.

The crack made by Duchess spread out in all directions, but it was stopped from spreading (see illustration) by the first crack in the corner of the mirror—the crack made by this decorator Vera Hopewell when she dropped the mirror.

Mr. Finney said that legally Duchess could not be held responsible for breaking a mirror that was already broken. (Mrs. Hopewell confessed on her own and will pay for the mirror.)

But Will and I couldn't get Duchess off the hook on the Chinese rug case. Duchess has been fired from the Finney household!

Sadly,

T*A*C*K

P.S. We enclose a picture of Duchess in happier days. Chuck thought it might cheer you up a little, but please send it back. He needs it.

Duchess on Trial

Afterword

The T∗A∗C∗K team had outdone itself. We'd solved still one more problem. This time, however, we felt as if we'd won a battle, but lost the war!

There was no changing Mrs. Finney's mind. She was getting rid of Duchess. We asked everyone we knew if they needed a dog. We didn't want Duchess to end up in the Animal Shelter. "But who *needs* a mutt?" Chuck's mother said.

Will and I begged our own parents to take Duchess. Will's parents said, *"Absolutely not."* My parents said, *"No and that's final."*

T∗A∗C∗K had come upon the hardest case of all. It's hard to solve unhappiness—especially our own.

But sometimes people don't solve problems. Sometimes problems are solved by chance—by lucky things happening right at the last moment. And that's just what happened.

Since I always ask you to try to figure things out, you probably don't mind trying again. It's not really fair, but . . .

Chuck got a letter. Can you guess who wrote it and what it said? Can you guess how _good luck_ solved this problem . . . before you turn the page?

Duchess on Trial

Conclusion:

SANDY HARBOR, AUGUST 11—

When Will and I arrived at Chuck's house, he was sitting on the lawn hugging Duchess. They both looked happy. Chuck handed me the letter. The postmark on the envelope said Pleasantville, but I didn't recognize the handwriting. I turned the envelope over. The return address said "Miles Pinkwater."

"That's Abby's father!" I gasped. "You read it, Will."

Will opened the letter and read it out loud:

Dear Chuck:

Abby showed me a picture of your puppy, Duchess. She is a lovely creature. I could be mistaken, but I am almost positive she is a pure-bred dog—a Great Pyrenees, to be exact.

Great Pyreneeses are hard to find. They come from an ancient breed that guarded livestock in the mountains between France and Spain. There are a few Great Pyreneeses in Pleasantville that are used as sheep guard-dogs. They protect the sheep from predators—wild animals and stray dogs that attack sheep. They do a very good job. They seem to have an instinct for it. A puppy would need very little training.

I also heard the bad news—that you are forced to give Duchess up. I know how much Duchess means to you, and I'd like to make you (I mean, Duchess) an offer.

A puppy like Duchess would be most valuable to me on the sheep farm I just bought. I would like to have Duchess here to train as a sheep-guarding dog. A Great Pyrenees is an independent dog. It does not really work for the farmer. It is not a herding dog. It lives out with the sheep—sleeping with them, eating with them, and taking care of them. The dog almost becomes part of the flock.

I must warn you that Duchess would be a working dog. She would not be Abby's dog; she would not be a household pet. You might say that a sheep-guarding dog does not really belong to anyone. Duchess would belong to the sheep.

Abby is very excited at the idea. She is jumping all over me right now.

In any case, it would be a pleasure to have Duchess with us. I think she will be happy. I look forward to hearing from you soon.

With best wishes,

Miles Pinkwater

"What do you think?" Chuck grinned. "Duchess has a job!"

When Chuck's mother read the letter, she sighed. "Duchess *is* a lovely creature," she said.

We stared at her.

". . . but, of course, we can't keep her," Mrs. Finney went on. "We must let her follow her natural instinct, but it *is* nice to have our dog recognized and appreciated for what she is."

Chuck was quiet for a moment. Then he said, "Amazing!"

"What's amazing?" I asked.

"Just think," Chuck said slowly. "If Duchess lives with the sheep, day and night, her name won't be Duchess anymore. The sheep will have their own name for her."

Will and I smiled at Chuck and Duchess. We had never seen them so happy.